The Siege of Cobb Street School

On the last day of term things are pretty boring, and the morning is passing very slowly. So Lenny and Jake decide to skive off to the cloakroom for a quiet bag of crisps. . . . And that's how they manage to escape the gunmen who just walk in and hold Miss Pritchard's class to ransom.

What are Lenny and Jake to do? Can they find a way of evading the gunmen and rescuing their classmates?

This is Hazel Townson's second exciting adventure story about Lenny and Jake — they also appear in *The Great Ice-Cream Crime*, published by Beaver.

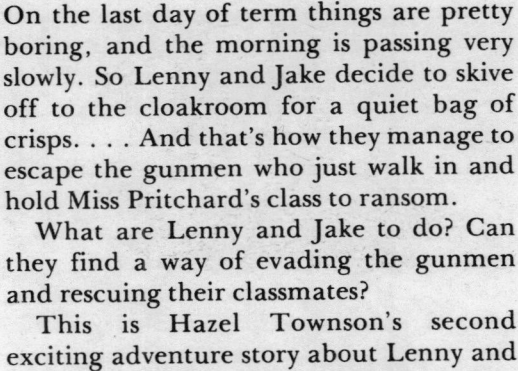

Also in Beaver by
Hazel Townson

The Siege of Cobb Street School

Hazel Townson

Illustrated by Philippe Dupasquier

Beaver Books

For my lovely new family —
My son's wife Christine and
My daughter's husband David

A Beaver Book

Published by Arrow Books Limited
62-65 Chandos Place, London WC2N 4NW

An imprint of Century Hutchinson Ltd

London Melbourne Sydney Auckland
Johannesburg and agencies throughout
the world

First published by Andersen Press Limited 1983
Beaver edition 1984
Reprinted 1986

Printed and bound in Great Britain by
Anchor Brendon Limited, Tiptree, Essex

ISBN 0 09 936650 9

1

It was the last day of term. Only Miss Pritchard's class was in school, because all the others were out on their end-of-term excursions. Miss Pritchard's class had had its excursion yesterday, to collect its prize in the Young Observer Collage Competition. The magnificent winning collage, mounted on thick board, now hung proudly on the classroom wall.

After yesterday's excitement there was an air

of anti-climax. School seemed half-dead without the other classes—just when a spot of boasting could have been quite enjoyable, too. No morning assembly; no proper lessons; just a long, boring wait until noon, when the main summer holiday would begin.

Miss Pritchard was reading a story. After that it would be playtime. Then a quick general knowledge quiz, and the great rush to freedom.

Lenny Hargreaves stifled a yawn. He had already watched a version of this story on television and knew how it would end. Trust old Pritty to pick one like that! Lenny began to daydream about his latest magic trick. The Flying Paperclips, it was called. You threw a handful of loose paperclips into the air and let them fall into an empty paper bag. You shook the bag, said the magic words, and hey presto!—you drew out the paperclips all fastened together in a long line. Really spectacular! He was going to use it as his opening trick at his forthcoming Charity Show in his dad's garage.

Lenny was rudely awakened by a kick on the ankle from his friend, Jake Allen, who sat right behind him. He turned to scowl at Jake, who gave him a slow and solemn wink. Then Jake's hand shot up.

Miss Pritchard sighed. 'Yes, Jake, what is it?'

'Please may I fetch Lenny a glass of water, Miss? He's not feeling too good.'

Lenny began a startled shout of protest, but it came out more like a croak. Miss Pritchard, fearing the worst, sent Lenny out at once to get a drink and a breath of fresh air, and asked Jake to look after him.

'How about that? Worked a treat!' Jake shouted gleefully when they were out of earshot.

'Rotter! Suppose I'd been listening to the story?'

'Well, you weren't. I could almost hear you snoring. Anyway, it's been on telly. Everybody knows how it ends.'

'Liar, then, saying I was ill when I'm not.'

'I didn't say you were ill. I said you weren't feeling too good, meaning angelic. When did you last feel angelic, Lenny Hargreaves?'

'All right, Clever Clogs, what do we do now?'

'Come on, we'll sit on the pipes in the cloakroom. I've got some crisps in my anorak pocket.'

It was from the cloakroom window that Jake spotted the two men crossing the school playground in a hurry. They were dressed in boiler-suits and carried plumbers' bags.

'If you want a drink you'd better be quick. It looks as though the plumbers have come to

turn the water off.'

'You'd think they could have waited until we'd all gone home.'

'My mum say workmen do it on purpose.'

'Do what?'

'Make everything as inconvenient as possible. She says it gives them a kick.'

'Yeah, like bus drivers who see you coming and won't wait.'

'They've gone down to the boiler-house,' reported Jake, still at the window.

'Huh! Why couldn't the boiler go out of action in the middle of the winter term, so we'd all get sent home! Just our luck!'

'Never mind, have some crisps.'

The two boys sat munching contentedly, never dreaming of the crisis that was about to transform their lives. For how could Jake and Lenny have guessed that the two 'plumbers' were already taking out guns from their plumbers' bags? Or that in a couple of minutes' time those two men would be creeping carefully along by the wall towards the door of Miss Pritchard's room?

2

Miss Pritchard's story was drawing to a close. Her voice had slowed down because she was trying to keep everyone guessing. Suspense, that was the important ingredient of storytelling. She noted with satisfaction that her method worked, too. Some of the class had been fidgeting quite brazenly all through the story, but were now sitting perfectly still, eyes wide, ears strained. She smiled, allowing a short, dramatic pause.

11

It was then that Miss Pritchard became aware of the draught from the door behind her. She was aware of a presence, too. Someone had opened that door, and now stood at her back. In fact, it was this someone who had caused the class to pay so much attention. They were not listening to the story at all.

Miss Pritchard turned . . . to see a man in a boiler-suit, pointing a long-barrelled gun at the class. The man advanced into the room, revealing a second man behind him. The second man's gun was aimed right at Miss Pritchard's head.

Miss Pritchard stared, feeling just as confused and speechless as the class.

'All right,' said the first man, whose name was Stone. 'Do as you are told, and nobody will get hurt. We just want you to sit nice and still for half an hour or so, while we make a couple of telephone calls. After that, with a bit of luck, you can all go home as usual.'

Miss Pritchard took a deep breath.

'I don't know who you think you are, but this is no sort of joke to play on young children. If

this is some students' rag . . . .'

The second gunman, whose name was Dagget, moved forward.

'Save your breath, love,' he said quite kindly. 'It won't make any difference.'

Miss Pritchard had no intention of saving her breath.

'Put that gun away at once! And stop frightening these children. Are you completely irresponsible?'

'No, as a matter of fact, we're not,' Stone replied patiently. 'We're here for a very responsible purpose. I've told you, nobody will be hurt if you do as we say. All we want is to save a friend of ours from serving a long prison sentence for something he didn't do. That's not irresponsible, is it?' He appealed to the class. 'You'd stick up for *your* friends if they were in trouble, wouldn't you?'

''Course they would!' Dagget answered for the petrified children.

'I see!' said Miss Pritchard grimly. 'You think you can use us as hostages to help you get your own way, is that it?'

'Full marks!' Stone smiled at the class. 'She's clever, your teacher.'

Miss Pritchard looked positively thunderous.

'I call that irresponsible, and a lot besides. Anyway, if you must have a hostage, you can have me. These children are all expected home at just after twelve, and if they don't turn up . . . .'

'Exactly!' Stone smiled again, like a man-eating tiger looking forward to its dinner. ''Cause quite a panic, wouldn't it?'

'You mean you are going to keep all these children here indefinitely?' Two pink spots began to burn angrily in Miss Pritchard's cheeks. 'Well, of course, you'll never get away with it.'

'Oh, I don't know! It's surprising what people get away with these days. Hi-jackings, bank robberies, assassinations; sieges and sit-ins and snipings. Besides, we're not asking for much. Just the release of our friend, a helicopter to get him away, and enough money for our escape. We're not greedy. It shouldn't take long to arrange, either, once we start the telephoning. Now, why don't you just relax? Take it easy, do as we say, and we'll all come out of it smiling!'

As he said this, Stone began to retreat towards the doorway.

'All right,' he told Dagget, 'I'll go and make those calls now. Any trouble and you know what to do.'

Dagget nodded, closing the door after Stone and stationing himself in front of it.

'Right!' he smiled round at the class. 'No

reason why you shouldn't get on with your lessons while you're waiting. It'll help to pass the time.'

Miss Pritchard scowled at the clock. 'It happens to be playtime.'

'All right, play, then. At your desks, of course. No moving about.'

'These children need to move about. They've been sitting still since half-past nine. They need exercise and fresh air and . . . .'

Dagget suddenly turned nasty.

'Look, lady, I've heard enough from you. Either you do as you're told, or somebody's going to get hurt. Is that clear?'

Somewhere at the back of the room a child began to whimper.

3

Lenny Hargreaves looked at his watch.

'It's five minutes into playtime. Where is everybody?'

'Looks like that story's still dragging on.'

'More likely everybody's fallen asleep.'

'Shall we go back and wake them up?'

'Not likely! I'm having my full quarter of an hour.'

The crisps were all eaten, so they started on a ball of chewing-gum which Lenny had found in a corner of his hanky. The chewing-gum was tasteless. What's more, playtime came and went with still no sign of the class.

'Do you suppose Pritty's let everybody go home early?'

'No chance! Still, something must be up. Let's go and peer through the windows.'

'It's a miracle she's not sent somebody to look for us by now. We could both be lying dead.'

'Forgotten all about us, I shouldn't wonder.' Lenny sounded hurt.

The two boys crept along by the wall, much as the gunmen had done, until they reached the outside of Miss Pritchard's classroom. Cobb Street Junior School was old, and the dark stone windowsills were high. There were, however, certain well-known footholds underneath, which Jake stepped neatly into.

Five seconds later he was dragging Lenny excitedly back towards the cloakroom.

'It's a hold-up! There's this bloke with a gun. Lucky he didn't see me. I think it's one of those plumbers.'

19

'Ha ha! Very funny!' sneered Lenny.

'No, honestly!' Jake described in detail the scene he had just glimpsed through the classroom window. He was so upset that Lenny reluctantly began to believe him. After all, the rest of the class still hadn't appeared.

'Let me have a look!'

'Don't be daft, he might see you!'

'Well, we can't just hang about. We've got to *do* something.'

'Raise the alarm.'

'Ring the police, you mean? They'll never

believe us. Remember what happened that time we found the bag of money?'

'They won't know who we are. We'll go to the office and dial 999. If we ask for fire, police and ambulance something's bound to turn up. They won't dare ignore us in case it really is an emergency.'

'I wouldn't bet on it. They'll be able to tell how old we are. Police never believe anyone under twenty-one. Pity Mrs Gladstone's away on the school trip. She could have done it.' Mrs Gladstone was the school secretary.

By now they were nearing the office, but Jake suddenly pulled up. He could see, through the half-open office door, a gunman standing there with the telephone in his hand. Luckily, the gunman had his back to the door.

'Oh, come on now,' Stone was saying, 'that's not much of a price to pay for a teacher and twenty-eight kids.'

Jake felt weak with horror as he realised what was happening. Suspicions were all very well, but now they knew for sure. They'd have to think fast. He shooed Lenny silently into the

room opposite the office, which happened to be the staff-room.

'Out of sight, quick!'

At the back of the staff-room was an ancient wardrobe, which seemed to be the handiest place to hide.

'Did you hear what he said?' whispered Jake from behind Miss Pritchard's voluminous macintosh.

'Yes. Holding us to ransom, then.'

'It's a siege!'

'And to think we wouldn't have been here at all today if we hadn't won a prize with our rotten collage.'

After a long, gloomy silence, Lenny said: 'It's all up to us, then, isn't it? We've got the only advantage. Those gunmen don't know we're here. Twenty-eight kids, I heard him say. But there are thirty of us. Maybe we can take them by surprise.'

'Us and who else?' Jake muttered glumly.

4

Miss Pritchard was not an easy enemy. Nearing retirement after a lifetime of teaching, she was wise in the ways of errant youngsters, and particularly bullies. The gunmen might think themselves grown-up, but to Miss Pritchard they were still youngsters misbehaving in a childish and particularly unacceptable fashion. If they thought they could scare her, they were very much mistaken.

Miss Pritchard was a bulky woman, with

two chins and a lot of tightly-permed grey hair. Her nickname, like most people's, was the opposite of the truth. She was not, and never had been, pretty, but there are other qualities more valuable than good looks in a crisis.

'All right, children,' said Miss Pritchard briskly, 'we'll carry on with the general knowledge quiz. Divide yourselves up into the usual four teams, A B C and D. I'll keep the score on the blackboard. Fiona, for goodness' sake stop snivelling. You don't know when you're lucky, my girl. Think of the tale you'll have to tell when you get home today. You'll be the centre of attention.'

Fiona stopped snivelling and wiped her eyes on her cardigan sleeve.

'Right, Barry, we'll begin with you. What is the capital city of Sweden?'

'Er—Stockholm, Miss.'

'Right! One point for team A.' Miss Pritchard marked up the score. 'Now, Jane. Which is the longest river in the world?'

The quiz picked up speed and the children became interested. Some of them were so

proud of their correct answers that they even stole sideways glances at the gunman to see if he appreciated their cleverness.

But Dagget had other things on his mind. He wished Stone would hurry up with the telephoning. He wished he could already hear that helicopter landing on the playing field behind the school. He wished the whole thing was over, and they were all safe in their hideout in the south of France.

Dagget was restless. He shifted his feet. Then he took a few paces away from the door towards

Miss Pritchard's desk. That made him feel uneasy because he had left the door unguarded, so he went back and wedged a chair under the doorknob. After that, he walked over to the teacher's desk and leaned against it, feeling that from here he had a better view of the class. That was when he glanced at the attendance register. It lay open at that day's date, with the newly-inked attendance ticks against the column of names. Idly, Dagget counted the ticks. There were thirty. Then he counted the children. Twenty-eight.

A small alarm-bell sounded in Dagget's brain. He counted the ticks again. Still thirty. Then he checked the date. Finally he counted the children again. Still twenty-eight.

Dagget picked up the register and slapped it hard against the side of the table to attract attention.

'Where are the other two?' he shouted.

Miss Pritchard stiffened. 'I don't know what you mean.'

'You know all right. Don't mess me about, lady. Thirty kids came in here this morning.

Now there are only twenty-eight. So where are the other two?'

'Oh, I see!' Miss Pritchard thought quickly. 'I sent one boy home sick, and another went with him. You don't send a sick child out alone.'

Dagget pointed at one of the boys in the front row.

'You! Is that right?'

The boy looked at Miss Pritchard, who stared straight back at him, chin held high.

'Yes, that's right.'

'If I find out anyone's been lying to me, the whole class is going to suffer.' Dagget pointed at another child. 'You! Who was sick?'

'Lenny Hargreaves.'

Dagget checked the register. 'Where's he live?'

The child he was questioning looked at Miss Pritchard, who gave an almost imperceptible nod.

'Number four, Pilling Street.'

'How far away's that?'

'Just by the railway station.'

'Right! We'll soon find out if he *has* gone home, and if he hasn't, then woe betide the lot of you.'

'You will not threaten these children!' cried Miss Pritchard angrily. 'I, and I alone, take responsibility for decisions made in this classroom.'

Dagget grinned nastily. 'Not now you don't, love!'

At that moment there were three sharp warning raps on the door—a prearranged signal—and Dagget had to hurry to let Stone in.

Stone looked very pleased with himself.

'Okay, that's it! Everything's in motion. All we have to do now is wait.'

'They'll send the helicopter and everything?'

'Haven't much choice, mate, have they?'

Dagget was so relieved he felt like hurdling over every desk in the classroom. It was all working out as Stone had said it would. It was actually happening! They were going to get away with it, and nothing could stop them now. Even the thought of the two missing children paled into insignificance. After all, the railway station was at least a mile away.

All the same, Dagget would have mentioned this to Stone if the next quiz question had not been punctuated by the sound of an approaching siren. The police were here. That thought drove all others from Dagget's mind.

5

It was dusty in the staff-room wardrobe. Lenny Hargreaves, huddled on the floor with an old fur bootee kicking him in the ribs, was in agonies trying not to sneeze. Luckily, since most of the staff were out there was only Miss Pritchard's coat in there, but a line of abandoned cardigans and sagging jackets hung just above the boys' heads, whilst all around them lay pairs of shoes in various stages of shapeless old age.

Jake had his eye to the crack in between the doors.

'Coast's clear,' he whispered at last. 'Shall we make a dash?'

'Where to?'

'Telephone.'

'No need,' Lenny pointed out. 'You heard him ringing somebody up. The whole world will know by now. That's the whole idea. He *wants* them to know, so that he'll get his ransom or whatever.'

'Well, we could escape out the back way.

33

Run home across the playing fields.'

'And leave Pritty and the others to their fate? Jake Allen, I'm ashamed of you!'

'I meant we could fetch reinforcements.' Jake was rattled because his courage was in doubt. 'You don't seriously think we can rescue them ourselves, single-handed?'

'Double-handed. We're the only chance they've got. The police will have all the reinforcements they want, but they can't do anything in case our kids get shot. But like I said, with the gunmen not knowing we're here, we could take them by surprise.'

'We'd have to have some weapons,' Jake retorted gloomily. Then he had a thought. 'Hey, suppose they've left more guns and stuff in the boiler-house? That's where they went first with those plumbers' bags.'

'I suppose it's worth a try,' agreed Lenny, edging the door carefully open and taking in a welcome gulp of stale staff-room air.

Slowly and cautiously the two boys crept from the staff-room down an assortment of corridors and out into the playground. After a final quick dash down a flight of stone steps they found themselves in the boiler-house.

'Dare we put the light on? I can't see a thing.'

'Yes, it won't show from the outside.'

Jake clicked the switch, and at once the two plumbers' bags were revealed in the middle of the boiler-room floor. But the bags were empty.

'Huh! Right waste of time that was! I don't suppose they'll even come back for these, so it's no use planning an ambush.'

Lenny began foraging around in a corner.

'There are plenty of weapons here, anyway.' He pointed out a shovel, a poker, a rake, some rope, an old football-net and a length of lead pipe. The shovel was so heavy he could only just lift it.

'What do you suppose we're going to do with those? We're nowhere near tall enough to bash anyone over the head unless they're lying down, and I wouldn't fancy it anyway. I'm a pacifist, me! Our best hope is to trick them. Use our brains, not our brawn.'

'All right then, you think of a trick!'

'A nice bit of magic, that's what we could do

35

with,' reflected Jake. 'Hey, what about one of your conjuring tricks or something?'

'You WHAT?' cried Lenny incredulously. Up to this moment, Jake Allen had steadfastly refused to have anything to do with Lenny's conjuring tricks, which he regarded with a mixture of amusement and scorn. Lenny felt both grateful and proud at this sudden change of heart. Now it was up to him to show Jake just how good he was.

At this point, Lenny remembered that all his conjuring stuff was at home.

6

Gun at the ready, Stone crouched by a corner of the classroom window, listening to the police loud-hailer blaring from the far side of the playground.

'All right, Stone, we've done as you asked. There's a helicopter on its way to pick up your friend and the money, then it will land on the playing field. It should be there in an hour and a half. So why don't you let those children go? We've got the vicar here, offering to come in as a hostage in their place. How about it?'

Stone sneered disdainfully. How soft did the police think he was? A classful of kids gave a lot better bargaining power than one middle-aged vicar.

For answer, he fired a single shot through the window, taking a notch out of a chestnut-tree in the front drive.

Fiona Crompton looked like starting to cry again, but Miss Pritchard hastily barked out a question she knew Fiona could answer and the moment of crisis passed.

'Team B are now leading by three points, thanks to Fiona, and I've got prizes for all those in the winning team, so the rest of you had better pull your socks up.'

Miss Pritchard had no idea what the prizes were to be, but no doubt she would think of something. The main thing just now was to keep the children's interest.

Suddenly an urgent hand shot up.

'Miss, please may I leave the room?'

There was an immediate flurry of hands.

'May I, Miss?'

'And me!'

'Me, too!'

Miss Pritchard glared defiantly at Dagget.

'Yes, of course, children. But one at a time . . . .'

Dagget, however, smiled and shook his head.

'No chance, lady! Nobody leaves this room except him and me. You've got a waste bin there. They'll have to use that.'

'I beg your pardon?' Miss Pritchard was outraged. 'They will do nothing of the kind! I never heard of such a thing!'

Dagget sighed patiently. 'If they want some privacy, pull that cupboard away from the wall and put the bin behind it.'

When Miss Pritchard began to protest some more, he snapped, less patiently, 'Look, missus, if that's the worst that happens to them, you'll be thanking your lucky stars before the day's out.'

'I wonder what *you* will be doing before the day's out?' reflected Miss Pritchard grimly. But she began moving out the cupboard, all the same.

Dagget nodded his approval. 'That's more like it! Your job's to do as you're told—and to keep these kids happy until the helicopter gets here. After that, you can call us all the names you like.'

'Stone!' the police loud-hailer rang out once more. 'We want a word with the teacher. Let her come to the window and talk. We need to make sure those children are all right.'

Miss Pritchard immediately stopped what she was doing and began moving towards the window, but Stone grabbed her arm and held her back.

'No luck, lady. If there's any talking to be done, I'll do it.'

'Have you no feelings at all? There are parents out there, wondering what's happening,' she began in an earnest whisper.

'Get on with your quiz,' advised Stone. 'Why don't you ask 'em how to spell "surrender"?'

7

Lenny could not forget what Jake had said
about needing a touch of magic. If only his
conjuring stuff had been available! He was sure
he could have thought of something to distract
the gunmen's attention long enough for them
to be taken by surprise. And then he
remembered something.

'Hey, Jake! There *is* some of my conjuring
stuff here in school after all. Remember that
imitation plastic pool of blood that I use for the

sawing-your-thumb-off trick?'

'Oh, that!' Jake recalled. 'You were fooling about with it in class and Pritty confiscated it.'

'Right! So I'll bet it's still in her locker in the staff-room.'

Lenny was already on his way to look for this strange object when Jake asked:

'What use do you think that's going to be?'

Lenny began to explain, and Jake's face slowly brightened with hope.

'Hey, that's not a bad idea!'

It was certainly a daring scheme, but given a little luck it might just work.

'It's a case of do or die,' said Lenny. 'We haven't much choice, so we'd better get started.'

'You realise if it doesn't come off we could get shot?'

'It will come off,' Lenny assured him with all the confidence of the professional artist.

First they had to prise open Miss Pritchard's locker. They searched the staff-room for a suitable tool, and came up with a long, steel knitting-needle which eventually did the job.

'Great! There it is!' cried Lenny, rummaging in the locker and triumphantly lifting out the plastic dark red 'pool'. 'Now for that football-net we brought from the boiler-house. Just give me time to sort myself out in the cloakroom, then you go off and fetch help.'

Jake tried to swallow, but his mouth felt dry. He was suddenly very nervous. It was all right for Lenny Hargreaves, lying safe and snug on the cloakroom floor, but what about him, Jake Allen, having to go and tackle the gunmen face to face? He couldn't help wondering what it would feel like to get shot.

'Please let it work!' Jake prayed silently. 'Let them believe me, and I'll give up chewing-gum for ever.'

Then he took a deep breath and set off for Miss Pritchard's classroom.

Jake banged loudly on the classroom door.

'Miss Pritchard! It's me, Miss! Jake Allen. I can't open the door.'

This was not surprising, since Dagget had again wedged a chair under the door-handle.

Stone leapt from his place by the window, swinging his weapon towards the door. Dagget's face turned two shades paler as uneasy memories flooded back.

'It's all right,' said Miss Pritchard calmly. 'It's only the boy I told you about. The one who went off with the sick child.'

'What sick child?' Stone turned on Dagget. 'Did you know about this?'

'She said they'd gone home before we got here. Right to the railway station. I didn't think it mattered, so far away . . . .'

'In a job like this everything matters.'

Without relaxing his guard on the door, Stone spoke to Miss Pritchard. 'What's he up to, this kid?'

'Jake's come back to his class, that's all. He's not up to anything.'

'You never said he was coming back,' complained Dagget.

'I didn't think he'd bother, since it's the end of term, but he's evidently a conscientious boy. You'd better let him in. He can't just stand about in the corridor.'

'It's a trick!'

'Nonsense! He's only a child. Let me talk to him.' If Miss Pritchard could catch a glimpse of Jake she felt she would know at once whether he realised what was happening. If he did, she must warn him it was too dangerous to try to help.

'How did he get back into school?' Stone wanted to know. 'The police have this place surrounded. They wouldn't have let him in unless it was a trick.'

'Oh, dear! That serves me right for telling lies,' Miss Pritchard thought. Then Jake's

47

voice came even more urgently from behind the closed door.

'Lenny's passed out, Miss. He's hit his head on the corner of the washbasin. He's unconscious, Miss, and he's bleeding like mad. I can't make him hear me. I've been trying for ages.'

'All right, Jake, just a minute!' Miss Pritchard turned to Stone. 'There's your answer. They never left school at all. Well, you'll have to let me go and see to the child.'

'There was nobody about when I went to the 'phone. I tell you it's a trick. That door stays fastened.'

'How can it be a trick? Do you think the police—our marvellous British police—would use a child like that? You can hear the genuine panic in the boy's voice.' Miss Pritchard, remembering suddenly what a great little actor Jake Allen had turned out to be in the last school play, confronted Stone with renewed determination.

'Look, there's a child hurt out there. He may be bleeding to death. You surely wouldn't

want that on your conscience? You pretend to be so keen on people's rights, trying to save your friend from punishment for a crime he didn't commit. All right then, what crime has that child committed? He needs medical attention, and I shall see that he gets it.'

The class watched tensely, silently cheering their teacher on. Miss Pritchard had gone up in their estimation quite a lot in the last half-hour.

'Get back, woman!' Stone held the teacher as she tried to reach the door. At the same time, however, he gave a signal to Dagget. Carefully,

Dagget removed the chair, inched open the door and poked his gun into the corridor. Then he kicked the door wide, snatched Jake's arm and dragged him into the room. The door crashed closed again behind him.

Jake Allen looked very upset, and his appearance caused quite a stir of interest in the class. Had something really happened to Lenny Hargreaves? And if it had, did that mean an ambulance might come and rescue them all?

Jake repeated his story about Lenny banging his head and lying unconscious, and ended with a dramatic plea for help.

'Aren't you going to *do* anything, Miss?'

'Of course we are, Jake. But for the moment this man's in charge. You must wait for him to decide.'

At last Stone gave in. 'All right,' he mumbled to Dagget. 'Go with the kid and have a look. Keep him right in front of you, just in case.'

'I'll go,' said Miss Pritchard quickly, not liking the thought of that gun at Jake's back.

But Stone only told her once more to mind her own business and get on with her quiz.

'It's all right, Miss,' Jake said courageously. 'He won't shoot me because I'm telling the truth. He'll be able to see in a minute.'

Jake and Dagget disappeared, and surely enough, almost immediately, Dagget's voice was heard calling back to Stone.

'It's okay, this kid *is* hurt, I can see him.'

Miss Pritchard, not knowing whether this was good news or bad, resignedly picked up the threads of the contest.

'Let's see—where were we?' She glanced at the blackboard. 'Team C. Danny, your turn. How many Ls in "parallel"?'

'Four, Miss. No, two. I mean—three.'

Meanwhile, Dagget advanced with some caution towards the figure lying in the pool of 'blood' on the cloakroom floor. Satisfied at last that this was a genuine emergency, he relaxed his hold on Jake and moved in to take a closer look at Lenny. That was when Dagget slipped on the soapy patch Lenny had laid on the floor beside himself. Before Dagget recovered his

balance or realised what was happening, there were two boys leaping round him, and he found himself struggling in the meshes of the football-net on which Lenny had been lying.

8

The two boys were luckier than they could ever have hoped to be. Fate took a hand in their capture of Dagget, for as the gunman struggled in the net, he swung his head with a mighty crack into one of the metal cloakroom posts and knocked himself out completely. It was an accident so similar to the one they had invented for Lenny that it seemed to the boys like poetic justice.

'I'll bet that was meant to happen,' said

Lenny with satisfaction. 'Jolly well serves him right.'

'Do you think we've killed him?'

'Not a hope! He'll be round in a minute, then he might kill *us*. Quick, grab his gun and let's tie him to the pipes.'

They made good use of the rope they had found in the boiler-house, and Lenny turned his tie into a gag. Jake obediently picked up the gun, holding it gingerly at arm's length. He didn't trust instruments of violence.

The two boys started back down the corridor.

'Mind what you're doing with that thing!' Lenny complained in a whisper as Jake accidentally prodded him with the gun. 'Here, you'd better let me have it. I know how to handle weapons.'

Lenny was referring to the toy pistol which was part of his conjuring programme. He would fire it into the air until a handful of loose feathers floated down, to the great amusement of the audience. Very effective, if you got it right, which Lenny rarely did.

Jake was glad to hand over the gun. He needed to concentrate on calling out again when they reached the classroom door. After all, Lenny couldn't call out, as he was supposed to be dying. But Jake need not have worried; the moment for him to call out never came.

What happened instead was that Lenny, tiptoeing right up to the door and preparing to station himself behind it, tripped over his own dangling shoe-lace, stumbled into the door and jarred his elbow. The gun went off.

Mercifully, the barrel of the gun was pointing upwards. The bullet sped through the thin plywood panel of the door and straight towards the adjacent wall, where hung the huge, magnificent, prize-winning collage. Stone had already heard noises in the corridor and had hastened to the door. Now he leapt backwards at the sound of the shot. He was just in time to take the full force of the collage board on the top of his head as Lenny's bullet loosened the plaster round the hook.

Stone sank with a groaning sigh as the great board sandwiched him to the floor—(Stone cold, as Lenny Hargreaves might have said)— and the gun he had been holding slithered away across the polish towards Miss Pritchard's feet.

Plaster-dust, screams and confusion filled the air. Chairs fell and desk-lids clattered as the frightened class took cover. As for Miss Pritchard, she bent down in utter disbelief and timidly gathered up the gun. As soon as she realised that Stone was in no shape to grab it back again, she grasped the weapon more tightly and marched determinedly to the door to tackle the second gunman.

'I'm armed!' she yelled, thinking that Dagget was in the corridor. 'So you'd better put up your hands!'

Carefully she drew back the door, and Jake Allen walked in with his arms obediently raised. Behind him stood Lenny Hargreaves, staring at his gun as if it had turned into a deadly serpent.

'Are you—alone, boys?'

'It's all right, Miss, the other one's tied up.'

This news snapped Miss Pritchard back into firm control.

'Right, Lenny, you'd better give that to me!'

Miss Pritchard now had a weapon in each hand, and wondered what on earth she was going to do with them. In the end she laid them both across her desk while she rummaged in her bag for a plain white handkerchief.

'Here, Fiona, shake this out of the window as a signal to the police.'

Then she picked up one of the guns again and pointed it vaguely in the direction of the prostrate Stone and the door. One couldn't be too careful.

9

All at once the classroom was full of policemen and shouting, bounding, laughing, crying children. Miss Pritchard's face turned quite grey and she sat down quickly.

The policemen were followed by ambulance men and nurses, who draped blankets over the children and led them outside, one by one, to the main gates where a crowd of parents, sightseers and journalists was waiting. Cameras flashed, mothers wept, bystanders cheered and reuniting families collided. In fact, the noise and confusion were even worse out there than they had been inside the classroom.

'Well done, boys!' Miss Pritchard managed to smile at Jake and Lenny, who still hovered anxiously at her side. 'But don't ever try a mad scheme like that again. Suppose you hadn't managed to hit the collage board? Or suppose you'd hit it and it hadn't fallen?'

'I wasn't trying to hit it,' Lenny admitted uncomfortably. 'It was all an accident.'

'We didn't think of anything so ambitious,' agreed Jake. 'We were just lucky, especially with the first bloke.'

'Well, it wasn't all luck,' argued Lenny. 'There was my plastic bloodstain . . . .'

Jake gave Lenny a kick on the ankle and quickly steered the subject away from the dangerous question of Miss Pritchard's busted locker.

'Pity we missed that helicopter, though. I'd have loved to see it come down on our playing field.'

'Too true!' agreed Lenny. 'We'll never get a chance like that again.'

The teacher was amazed. 'Don't you two

boys think you've had enough excitement for one day?'

Lenny treated this question seriously.

'It depends what you mean by excitement, Miss. There's scared-excitement and there's fun-excitement. Helicopters are fun.'

'Maybe we could get cut off by the tide or something in the holidays,' suggested Jake. 'Then they'd winch us up.'

Miss Pritchard was quite sure that Jake Allen and Lenny Hargreaves could manage a simple thing like that. However, she said she had a better idea.

'They run helicopter pleasure trips from Spagley aerodrome. Suppose I were to take you both up for a treat?'

'Honest, Miss?'

'Will you really?'

'As a sort of prize for catching the gunmen?'

Miss Pritchard gasped. 'Prize? Oh dear, I've just remembered. I promised prizes to the winning team in the quiz, but I haven't anything to give them.'

Lenny put a hand into his pocket.

'Don't worry about that, Miss. You can give them all tickets for my next conjuring show. It's in my dad's garage on Sunday afternoon. All proceeds for charity, including sales of chewing-gum in the interval.'

At these words, Jake Allen groaned and slapped a hand to his forehead.

'And *I've* just remembered I've promised to give up chewing-gum for ever.'

'Well now,' smiled Miss Pritchard, 'that is the most pleasing bit of news I've heard all day.'

64